SOME SWELL PUP

SOME SWELL PUP
or Are You Sure You Want a Dog?

Story by Maurice Sendak and Matthew Margolis

Pictures by Maurice Sendak

A SUNBURST BOOK

MICHAEL DI CAPUA BOOKS

FARRAR, STRAUS AND GIROUX

For Connie, Erda, Io, and Aggie M.S.

For my son, Jesse M.M.

ONE HOUR LATER . . .

AND SO, NEXT DAY . . .

THAT NIGHT...

SO THEY WENT TO SLEEP AND DREAMED . . .

AND IN THE MORNING . . .

SO...